A Model Death

A Model Death

Brenda Chapman

Anna Sweet Mysteries
GRASS ROOTS PRESS

First published in 2014 by Grass Roots Press

Grass Roots Press gratefully acknowledges the financial support
for its publishing programs provided by the following agencies:
the Government of Canada through the Canada Book Fund and the
Government of Alberta through the
Alberta Foundation for the Arts.

Library and Archives Canada Cataloguing in Publication

Chapman, Brenda, 1955–, author
    A model death / Brenda Chapman.

(Anna Sweet mysteries)
ISBN 978-1-77153-007-1 (pbk.)

    I. Title. II. Series: Chapman, Brenda, 1955– . Anna
Sweet mysteries.

PS8605.H36M63 2014   C813'.6   C2014-906899-9

Printed and bound in Canada.

For my mom, Ollie Chapman

"It's not like Nick to be late." Jada Price, my partner at Storm Investigations, tilted her beer bottle so that it pointed toward our closed office door. "He said that he'd be here early to help celebrate."

"Something better must have come up." I rammed the knife hard into the Black Forest cake I'd bought at a bakery down the street. We were having a little party to mark the end of a big case—we'd reunited a missing teenager with her family after a year on the street. It looked like the kid was happy to be home and that felt good. What Jada didn't know was that our office assistant, Nick Roma, had asked me to dinner after the cake cutting.

I'd been looking forward to seeing if the spark I felt for him could grow into something deeper. But Nick must have had second thoughts about his offer. He could have at least called to let me know he was backing out.

"Refill your beer?" Jada asked as she pulled open the small fridge door.

"No thanks. I'm going to head out for a burger after this cake. You can come along if you like."

"I've got a date. Sorry."

Jada had a string of men eager to take her out. She rarely had to cook a meal or eat alone. I raised the knife and gave the cake another whack. Nick Roma was the only date I'd accepted since I'd come back to Ottawa the year before. Now he'd stood me up and I felt like a fool.

I flipped the piece of cake onto a plate and handed it to Jada. She looked from me to the knife and back again, but didn't say anything. I hacked off a second piece for myself before we took our chairs side by side, and put our feet up on the desk.

Jada scooped a forkful of icing into her mouth. She followed it with a swallow of beer and said, "I hear your sister Cheri is back in town."

"So I've been told."

"You haven't seen her?"

I shook my head. "It's complicated."

"Yeah, I guess."

"She missed Evan's seventh birthday."

I had mixed feelings about my flighty sister, mostly angry ones. What kind of mother left her family for a year to work overseas? Cheri's claim that she needed the time away to further her career had been the height of selfishness in my book. Evan and my brother-in-law, Jimmy, had coped okay after a few months of moping around. They'd both spent a lot of time at my dad's house, where I was staying. Maybe too much time.

Jimmy and I had been engaged before he took up with my sister and married her instead. I could tell the last few months that he was rethinking his choice. I hoped Cheri's return from China would get things back to normal. I'd also been hoping a date with Nick Roma would get my thoughts off Jimmy. So much for good intentions.

I ate the last of my slice of cake and stood up. "I'm heading out. If Nick shows up . . . tell him . . . tell him I couldn't wait any longer."

"Where are you having supper?"

"I'll wander up Wellington Street until I find a place."

I left the office and climbed down the stairs. When I reached the sidewalk, I walked west along the busy Hintonburg street, which was lined with stores, restaurants, and coffee shops. The evening was warm for October, but the summer had been a hot one. In daylight, the leaves were brilliant yellow, red, and orange. Some crunched under my feet but most were still on the trees. By now, though, the sun had sunk behind the tall buildings and the streetlights were on. Thanksgiving was just over a week away.

After I crossed Holland, I entered a pub called The Wood. The food was good and I could sit at the bar and watch sports on the flat screen. I ordered a pint of local beer and a cheeseburger platter.

The pretty bartender flicked through the stations on the television in front of me and stopped on a breaking news alert. She turned to me, her brown eyes wide. "Have you heard about this?"

"Heard about what?"

"One of the TV stars from the show *A Model Life* was murdered near the Rideau Canal. Dow's Lake, to be exact."

"No way." I leaned closer and she turned up the volume. The reporter's face was upset. She said into the camera, "Lena Caruso was found by a passing jogger early this morning. Police aren't saying much at this time but are asking for anyone with information to come forward."

A photo of a stunning Italian girl in her twenties filled the screen. A hotline phone number was just below her image. She had masses of long black hair, giant eyes the colour of dark chocolate, and high cheekbones. She'd been one of a trio of models from other countries being filmed as they adjusted to life in Ottawa. The reality show was a hit in the city and the three women were instant stars.

"What a tragedy," I said.

"Isn't it? Nobody is safe." The girl switched channels to a football game as my burger arrived.

My cellphone rang while I was popping the last French fry into my mouth.

"Nick's being held at the police station on Elgin. They say he murdered his girlfriend in a jealous rage and left her by the canal. Can you get down to the station and check it out?" Jada's voice was loud and worried.

"That can't be right," I said. My eyes returned to the television screen then back to my empty beer glass. I pictured Lena Caruso's beautiful face with the hotline number below. Nick had been a movie star in Italy before he moved to Ottawa to be with his dad. And he liked to keep his past a secret. If what Jada said was true, all that was about to change.

I signalled with my hand for the bartender to come over. "I'll get down there as soon as I can," I said to Jada.

"Good. Phone me when you know what's going on." The line went dead.

"Was everything okay with your meal?" The girl waited while I fished in my pocket for my wallet.

"It was great. But I have to cancel the beer I just ordered. I got called into work."

"I know what that feels like. All your plans go down the toilet."

"Yeah." *As if I'd had any plans to flush away.*

On the way back to my car, which I'd left parked near the office, I mumbled, "Stupid, stupid, stupid." What was it with me and men? The second I start letting one of them close to me, they end up being a murder suspect. I should never have let someone as secretive as Nick Roma into my world. Killer or not, he had enough baggage to fill an Ottawa city bus.

CHAPTER TWO

I walked into the Elgin Street police station twenty minutes later. It was going on seven thirty. I was pleased to see my old friend Carlo Sanchez working the main desk. We'd met when I was a cop several years earlier, before I shot and killed a drugged-out kid while on duty. Carlo had tried to convince me to stay on the force. He hadn't succeeded, but I'd always thought of him as a friend.

"Hey, Anna Sweet! I figured you'd be paying us a visit this evening."

I leaned against the desk and smiled. "I guess you know Nick Roma works for us. What can you tell me about the case?"

"Not much but Mr. Roma has been answering questions since early afternoon."

"Who's in there with him?"

"Ice Cube and your ex."

Translation: Detective Johnny Shaw and my brother-in-law, Jimmy Wilson.

"What's Jimmy doing on the case? He and Shaw don't work together."

"Jimmy asked to be on this one, and Shaw was down a cop." Carlo shrugged. "Cutbacks."

Of course Jimmy asked to be on this case. He'd disliked Nick from the moment he met him. They'd been like two bulls sizing each other up. "What have they got on Nick?" I asked.

"I don't know much. But Lena Caruso and Nick Roma go way back, apparently."

"The news report didn't say how she died."

Carlo searched the room with his eyes to make sure nobody was listening. He looked back at me. "Strangled. She was found in some bushes near Dow's Lake this morning around five o'clock."

"How long had she been dead?"

"They think anywhere between four and six hours." Putting time of death somewhere around midnight.

"Was she . . ."

"Raped? Not that I heard."

"Thanks, Carlo. Is Nick under arrest?"

"No, not yet. Unless he confesses, he should be out soon. You can wait over there if you like." He pointed to some chairs near the wall.

I took a seat and texted Jada with what little information I had. Then I scrolled through news sites on my phone to read more about the case. The papers had less facts than I'd gotten from Carlo. After a while, I put away my phone, stretched out my legs, and folded my arms across my chest.

"Wake up, Anna."

I opened my eyes and turned my head. Nick Roma was sitting beside me, a weary smile on his face. He wore jeans, a blue-and-white checked shirt, and tan leather shoes. His straight black hair was gelled back from his face and stubble darkened his cheeks. Even after a day of questioning, he looked and smelled good. His black eyes studied me. I saw sadness in their depths that he blinked away when he knew I was awake.

"What time is it?" I sat up and stretched.

"Nine thirty. Time to get out of here."

Nick didn't wait for me to pull myself together. I caught up with him just outside the station. He was standing to the left of the main entrance, looking at the full moon and breathing in the cool night air. I waited beside him until he turned and looked down at me. I could see the same tight smile he'd had on his face when I woke up.

"Do you need a lift?" I asked.

"If you don't mind. I could catch a cab if it's out of your way, though."

"I don't mind."

We started walking toward the crosswalk. My car was parked on a side street on the other side of Elgin. I didn't say anything, waiting for him to break the silence.

Nick stopped suddenly on the sidewalk, steps from my car. "I need to hire Storm Investigations," he said. "Because I'm in a lot of trouble." His face was a mix of pain and confusion.

My first instinct was to put an arm around his shoulders and give him a hug. My second was to smack him on the chest and ask him what he'd gotten himself into.

Instead, I clicked my key fob and unlocked the car doors. "Let's go get a drink somewhere," I said. "Then you can tell me all about Lena Caruso and why they think you killed her."

I didn't ask him if he had. There'd be time for that soon enough.

CHAPTER THREE

Nick had recently moved into a luxury town house that he owned backing onto the canal near the University of Ottawa. It was another strike against him in the murder investigation, since the canal fed into Dow's Lake. I drove north until I found a parking spot near the Elgin Street Diner. I turned off the engine and glanced over at him.

"You look like you need something to eat," I said. "I already ate but don't mind watching you have a meal."

"I'm starving, actually. And I'm sorry I missed taking you out for dinner."

"Don't even think about it. That's the least of your worries."

We took a booth at the back of the restaurant. Nick ordered a club sandwich and a beer, and I asked for a coffee. I took out my notepad after the waitress served our drinks.

"So tell me about Lena Caruso."

Nick rubbed a hand across his jaw. "I can't believe she's dead. The entire time the police were asking me questions, I thought they had the wrong woman. Lena was always so full of life and fun."

"If Jada and I are going to help you get out of this, you have to tell me everything."

Nick's sandwich arrived and he took a bite. He seemed to be buying himself some time. At last, he started talking.

"My father told you that I was an actor in Italy. I'd asked him not to share that information, but he likes to brag—I guess fathers always do." Nick smiled and shook his head at the thought of Gino. "My parents separated when I was ten and I moved with Dad to Canada when I was twelve. I went back to Rome to live with my mother when I was fifteen. She signed me up for a movie audition the next year and I got the part. That led to more movies and I became well known in Italy. I met Lena on the set of one when we were both eighteen. She was a model but acted in small parts. Soon we were dating, and then we lived together for a couple of years."

"Gino said that she broke your heart."

Nick's eyes held mine. "I told him that, but it wasn't true. I left her. Lena was scared people would think less of her, so I let everyone think she dumped me. We'd grown apart and had nothing in common anymore. I came home to spend time with Dad last year."

"But Lena followed you to Ottawa."

"Yeah. I think Lena felt that I'd regret leaving, given some time. She wanted us to make another go of it, so she had her agent search for work in Ottawa. He found this reality TV show and she tried out for it. She was perfect for the part."

"Did you spend time together after she arrived in Ottawa?"

Nick's eyes slid from mine and he took another bite of his sandwich. "She kept calling me. Every night for a month. I finally agreed to meet her in August. I told her we could be friends but nothing more. She stopped phoning . . . for a while."

"As I recall, she has a boyfriend on the show."

"The writer gave her one. It's not a real relationship."

"You've just killed my faith in reality TV."

"They work from a script, just like any other show. It's thinly disguised acting."

Now came the question I'd been dreading. "Did you meet Lena yesterday at Dow's Lake?"

Nick shifted in his seat so that he was looking over my shoulder. "She'd started calling again this week, leaving messages on my voice mail. The last few messages, I heard panic in her voice. I called back two days ago and Lena asked me to meet her. I agreed because she said she had nobody else to turn to. I thought she was making up a crisis, but couldn't be sure."

I repeated, "Did you meet her at Dow's Lake?"

"I arrived at Malone's Grill in the field house at Dow's Lake at ten last night and waited for her for an hour. But Lena never showed. I walked along the canal for a while and then drove home. She didn't answer any of my text messages."

"Ten seems kind of late." I kept my voice flat.

"She said she had stuff to do first."

"You have no idea why she was frightened?"

"None whatsoever. Looks like she had good reason to be afraid, though. I wish I'd been able to help her, but now it's too late."

I studied Nick's face but I didn't know him well enough to tell if he was lying. He hadn't revealed anything from his past life in all the months he'd worked for us. And I could tell he didn't like being forced to tell his secrets now. I wondered how bad this murder investigation would have to get before he told me everything.

Nick ate the last of his sandwich and I called the waitress over for our bill. It had been a long day and we needed to get some sleep to face whatever surprises were coming our way tomorrow.

••••••••••

Dad was still up when I got home at eleven thirty. He was sitting in his recliner in the living room, reading and sipping his nightly Scotch before bed. I plopped down in the chair next to his.

"You look like you've had a busy night," he said. "Work or fun?"

"Work."

"Too bad. You could use a hot date now and then. Keeps the energy levels up."

I gave him a sideways grin. "You go first."

"I just might." He closed his book and drained the last of his drink. "I've invited your sister and the family for Thanksgiving dinner. Jimmy should be able to make it."

"Dad, I was hoping to put off seeing Cheri for a while. I'm working on a new murder case now. So is Jimmy."

"You both have to eat. It's time for you and Cheri to bury your hatchets and get on with being sisters again. Neither one of you is perfect."

"What do you mean by that?"

"Maybe it's my fault. After your mother died, I wasn't always the best at that sympathy parenting stuff. I found it easier to ignore your girl troubles and all the drama. But both you and Cheri have the knack for running away when relationships get tough."

I thought about my five years waitressing in bars around the US and knew he had a point. I pushed myself to my feet. I was more tired than I'd been in a long time.

"Well, it'll be nice to see Evan . . . and maybe Cheri, too. I'm heading up to my room, Dad. I've just got to check out a website before I crawl into bed."

He saluted me with his right hand. "Sleep tight, kiddo. Remember, tomorrow's a shiny, brand new day."

....

Jada and I met in our office at eight a.m. I'd picked up coffee and muffins on the way and we took a minute to eat before we got down to it.

"This case I took on yesterday couldn't have come at a worse time," Jada said. "I agreed to follow a man to see if he's cheating on his wife. She wants an answer by the end of the month."

"I can handle Nick's case alone," I said. "No problem."

Jada's eyebrows went up, as if she didn't believe me.

"What?" I asked.

"Nothing." Jada took a sip of coffee. "Okay. You start checking out Lena's work situation and love life. I'll do some online research when I can. Let me know if you need me for something specific."

"Will do. I'm heading over to the set of *A Model Life* to talk to the other models and crew. I'll also talk to people in Nick's town house development, although I doubt any of them talk to each other. People with money don't like to be sociable as a rule."

"Cynic." Jada crunched up the wrapper from her muffin and tossed it in a high arc into the garbage.

"More like realist," I said. "Whenever I think someone's going to impress me, they always disappoint."

Jada searched my face. "Nick's not a bad guy," she said softly. "You have to keep the faith."

I stood and grabbed my jacket. "Faith has let me down too many times. I deal in facts now. They never lie or give false hope."

Jada shook her head but didn't say anything. She knew that I wasn't going to be easily talked out of my new world view.

CHAPTER FOUR

A Model Life was being filmed in a house in a section of the city called Kanata, in the west end. The two-storey, grey brick house sat on a big lot, although a three-car garage took up most of the front yard. The three models lived in the house and let a cameraman film their every move. The words "fish bowl" and "insanity" came to mind.

I was sorry to see Jimmy's squad car parked in the driveway. I thought about going for breakfast and coming back later. Thought about it, but realized I'd be running into Jimmy often if I was going to help Nick. *Be bold,* I told myself, and parked my car on the street in front of the house.

I started up the sidewalk and the front door opened. As my bad luck would have it, Jimmy and another detective stepped outside. Jimmy squinted in my direction before putting on aviator sunglasses. He ran a hand through his messy black curls and waited for me to reach him. The other detective headed for the car without looking back.

"Don't tell me you're working this," Jimmy said.

"Then I won't tell you."

I passed where he was standing at the bottom of the steps.

"You can't just waltz into this case, Anna. You aren't on the police force anymore."

"Nick Roma hired Storm Investigations. I have every right to interview people." I could feel my chin jut out and my anger begin to boil. "Someone has to make sure he gets a fair trial."

"Ouch." Jimmy pretended to jump back and clutched his chest. "Don't let Shaw hear you talking like that. He might take offence."

"It's more you I'm worried about getting the facts right."

Jimmy grinned at me and held out the hand he'd had on his chest. "Truce? I promise to deal fairly with Nick if you stop thinking the worst of me."

I looked at Jimmy's hand for a second before walking toward him and reaching out to take it. "Truce." I was going to need his cooperation more than he was going to need mine. I tried to pull my hand away, but he held on.

"How's Cheri?" I asked, my eyes on his.

"She's good." He frowned and dropped my hand. "See you around, Sweet."

"Yeah. See you around."

I watched him join his partner in the car before I turned and stepped inside model land.

I followed women's voices to a kitchen at the end of a long hallway. A large open space to my right was a living room and dining room area. Camera equipment and lights were everywhere. The furniture was modern and expensive—glass, chrome, and white leather in abundance. Latin tango music filled the space, from speakers hidden in the walls.

I recognized Ella Blom and Sang Hee Yum from the one time I'd watched the show. Ella was a tall Swede with long, white-blonde hair and blue eyes the size of quarters. Sang Hee was tinier, but no less beautiful, and from Korea. She had long black hair and a smile that lit up the room.

They looked up at me from the couch as I walked over. Both models' faces were sad and they had tears in their eyes. I introduced myself and sat on the chair across from them.

"A PI?" Sang Hee asked. "Are you for real?"

"I am, and I have a few questions if you're willing."

Ella shrugged, her mouth set in a grim line. "Sure, why not?"

"Let me first say how sorry I am for your loss." I paused for a moment of respect, then said, "When is the last time you saw Lena?"

Sang Hee answered first. "The evening she died. We were filming in the afternoon and had supper together afterward. We ordered in Chinese food. If we'd only known it would be our last meal together." She dabbed at her eyes with a tissue.

"Was she worried about anything? Acting strangely?"

Sang Hee shook her head. Ella frowned. "She'd been down all week but I figured it was her time of the month. She told me that she was thinking of leaving the show."

"Any reason?"

"None that she said."

Sang Hee looked at me as if she was remembering something. "I overheard her talking on the phone—I don't know to who—and she was upset. I asked her about it after, and she said that a man from her past was bothering her. I guess it was that Nick Roma guy."

Not good.

Ella said, "Lena liked the rich life. I was worried about her a bit."

Sang Hee nodded. "She was our party girl on the show. You know, the one who drank too much and said crazy things. She'd fight with her fake boyfriend even though he always acted totally in love with her. The script was getting sexier and they had some steamy scenes. She complained to the director but he said ratings were up."

Ella added, "The real Lena was kind and fun to be around. But she had secrets."

I never got to ask my next question. Both girls sat up straighter and stopped talking when two tall men entered the room. They had the self-important look of people in charge. The rest of the television crew trailed in behind them. One of the first two men walked over to stand in front of Ella and Sang Hee.

"Hi John," Ella said. "I don't think we're up for filming today."

John Shore, the director. I'd found his name on the show's website the night before.

Shore nodded as if he understood. The expression on his face was sad and sincere enough to make me think he cared about their grief. "I know this is tough, girls. But we're going to film your reaction to Lena's death . . . for the fans. Raymond has quickly put together a script." He pointed to the other tall man, now standing behind him with a stack of papers in his hands. Raymond had a shaved head and wore a suit jacket over a white T-shirt and jeans. He was staring at me with curious eyes. Shore's voice got harder, not allowing for any argument. "You can read it over while we set up." Then he spotted me. "And you would be . . . ?"

"Anna Sweet. I'm one of the investigators." *Let him think I'm with the police.*

Shore's pale blue eyes challenged me before he looked over at Ella and Sang Hee. He had a face pitted with acne scars that a full beard didn't quite hide. His hair was straight and brown and reached his shoulders from under a black baseball cap. He looked fit inside his tight T-shirt. Without looking at me, he finally said, "Fine, but don't get in the way."

Raymond handed out the sheets of paper to the models. Neither looked happy with the assignment. I could hardly stomach it myself.

By now, a cameraman, a lighting guy, a makeup artist, and a hairstylist were busy getting the set and the actors ready. Raymond was standing alone near the gas fireplace. I walked over and stood next to him.

"Is it hard writing for models?" I asked.

He pushed his black-rimmed glasses further up his nose and laughed. "It might have been, but these models are smart as well as beautiful." He had the trace of a French accent.

"What will you do now that Lena's gone?"

Instantly, his face became serious. "We put a call out for a new actress this morning. The show must go on, even though we're all devastated by Lena's death."

"Murder," I said. "Lena's murder."

The muscle in his square jaw jumped. "Right, yes. Thank goodness they've caught the guy who did it."

"And who would that be?"

"Her ex-boyfriend. Nick somebody. I heard he confessed to stalking her."

I decided to play along. "Did Lena say she was being stalked?"

Raymond nodded his bald head. "She told me a few days before she died."

"What exactly did she say?"

Raymond took a step closer and spoke quietly into my right ear. "Lena said someone from her past wouldn't leave her alone. She was scared, I can tell you that. I guess now we know that she had a reason to be."

"Did she actually say it was Nick Roma?"

"Not in so many words. But we all knew he was trying to get her back."

CHAPTER FIVE

I checked in with Jada before I headed over to Nick's neighbourhood. "Not looking good," were my first words. "Everyone in the model house seems to think Nick was actively pursuing Lena. He's the only one who says it was the other way around."

Jada snorted over the phone. "I believe Nick over the others any day."

"How can you be so sure?" After all, we'd only known Nick for just over a year. He'd been a good worker but hadn't shared much about himself. We couldn't be blinded by how attractive he was. Only trouble lay in that direction.

"Because I think he had his sights set on someone else."

My heart fell. Nick probably had brought a woman to the office when I wasn't there. I forced myself to ignore my disappointment and focus on the case. "Well, whatever. I'm going to see if any of Nick's neighbours saw anything that could help with an alibi."

"Good idea. As for my following-the-husband update, I'm about to leave my car and tail him into Herongate Mall. So far, he's been to the gym and had coffee at Starbucks. No cheating as of yet."

"Let's hope your case has a happy ending. Because I'm seriously beginning to doubt that Nick's will."

··········

Nick's three-storey town house stood on a street lined with identical structures. Each had a small yard but the more expensive ones had a view looking onto the Rideau Canal. I knocked on four doors before a young woman in stretchy workout clothes answered. She lived in the town house directly across the street from Nick's place.

"Most people are at work now," she said after looking at my ID. She wiped sweat from her forehead with a pink towel. "Yeah, I know Nick to see him. I mean, how can you not notice the guy. He's drop dead gorgeous." Her eyes widened. "I didn't mean any offence when I said 'drop dead.'"

"None taken," I said. I held up my iPhone to show her a photo of Lena Caruso. I'd uploaded it from the internet. "Did you ever see this woman with Nick?"

"She's the one who was . . . no. I never saw her aside from on the TV show. What a shame about her murder."

"Did you happen to notice any of Nick's comings and goings two nights ago?"

"I saw his car pull out after I finished with my trainer. It would have been going on ten o'clock. I didn't see Nick come home, though. I was out for a jog and stopped by a friend's place."

"So you have no opinion about Nick Roma one way or the other."

"Well, he always seemed like a nice guy. No women or wild parties. I never would have believed in a million years that he'd kill anyone."

"Okay. Thanks for your help."

I wasn't sure if Nick was home but I crossed the street and pressed on his doorbell. I was almost relieved when he didn't answer. It was time to head back to the office and do some research on my computer.

I drove the side streets back to Wellington and found a parking spot in front of a used clothing store.

On my walk to our office, I passed by Roma's Pizza Shop, which took up the bottom floor of our building. Gino was behind the counter, waving one arm in the air as he spoke on his cellphone. I slipped past the window without him seeing me. I wasn't up for his questions about how I was going to prove that Nick was innocent. I'd have had to make up something to stop him from worrying about his son's chances.

I climbed the stairs and found the office door locked. Happily, I would have the place to myself. It crossed my mind that Nick wasn't at home or at work. I wondered where he might be but didn't let myself worry about him. My energy would be better spent working on his defence.

The first thing I did was a Google search on Lena Caruso. A number of articles popped up and I started reading about her early years in the movie industry. The reviews were not good. "Can't act." "Beautiful but wooden." "She should stick to modelling." The first movie she'd acted in when she was eighteen, with Nick Roma, had been a success. Nick received great praise for his role as an Italian student, but reviewers had not been kind to Lena. I imagined how crushing that must have been for her.

There were several articles about Nick and Lena as a couple, along with pictures from different social events. They were truly two of the beautiful people. One article announced their breakup after two years together. Nick was quoted as being devastated.

Lena didn't make any movies for the next few years, although she kept modelling. She was in the big fashion shows and in several magazines. From what I could tell, she was travelling to shoots in exotic locations right up to her death. *A Model Life* was her first big acting role in a long time. I found the last few episodes online and settled in to watch.

I'd just finished viewing the last show when I heard footsteps on the stairs. A few seconds later, Jada burst into the office. She threw her bag on the desk and flopped into the chair next to me.

"What a day. I've been all over the place following the husband. I almost thought he was innocent but he's disappointed me. I have pictures of him meeting another woman outside a motel. I kept wishing it wasn't so, but they went inside one of the rooms together."

"Too bad," I said. "But not unexpected. Most men cheat." *If Jimmy Wilson is anyone to go by.*

Jada rolled her eyes at me. "Where did that come from? You used to believe in love."

"Let's say that I had an awakening when my fiancé made out with my sister." I turned the computer screen toward her. "By the way, have you seen any episodes of *A Model Life*?"

"I love that show. It's so corny that I can't stop watching."

"I don't get the attraction of reality TV. They treat these models like sex objects. Do you know they even filmed them having a shower? Lena is shown with that pretend boyfriend in some very intimate scenes."

"That's half the fun." Jada frowned. "But now that you mention it, I suppose they do treat women terribly."

"Has Nick ever talked to you about Lena or his acting career?"

"Nope."

"Strange." I stood and stretched. "I'm heading home. What are you up to tomorrow?"

"I'll be following the husband another day or two as I agreed to do in my contract with his wife. I'll check in."

"Where's Nick?"

Jada looked around as if she might find him hiding in a corner. "I told him to lay low for a few days while you sort this out. He said he has faith that you'll uncover the truth."

"I really hope he's not going to be disappointed."

Especially if the truth is that he killed his ex-girlfriend.

CHAPTER SIX

Dad had left a note saying that he was at his ballroom dancing lesson. I'd find a plate of meatloaf and potatoes in the fridge with my name on it. He'd drawn a big happy face wearing tap shoes at the bottom of the page.

I was humming as I heated up my supper in the microwave. I thought about Dad's unusual new hobby. The owner of the dance studio was the daughter of one of Dad's army buddies. She'd asked him to come out because they were short of male partners. So my grumpy dad, who had never danced a step as long as I knew him, was now dressing up, putting on aftershave, and trotting down to Bank Street a couple of nights a week. Climate change wasn't the only major shift going on in the world.

My cellphone rang as I was climbing into bed. I leapt over to where I'd left it on the dresser and clicked the receive button.

"I hear you're making yourself into a pest."

I caught my breath, then said, "And a good evening to you too, Shaw." Jimmy must have told him that I was working for Nick. "Kind of late for you to be calling."

I could hear Detective Shaw's loud sigh in my ear. "Come by the station tomorrow morning before nine, Sweet. We may as well fill you in on what we've got so you don't keep getting in the way."

I smiled. "I'll set my alarm."

"You do that." Shaw clicked off without wishing me a good night.

· · · · · · · · · ·

The rain was pouring down when I left Dad's Alta Vista home the next morning to drive to the Elgin Street police station. I parked and dodged puddles as I made my way to the main entrance. A gusty wind knocked leaves from the trees and swirled them around my feet as I ran.

Jimmy and Shaw were in Shaw's office drinking coffee when I arrived, shaking rain from my hair and coat. Shaw pointed to the coffee pot near the window and I poured myself a cup before sitting down next to Jimmy. We took a moment to gulp some liquid caffeine before Shaw started talking.

"The first results from Lena Caruso's drug testing are back. She was high on cocaine at the time of her death. A large amount of the drug was in her system. Signs are that she was a regular user. She was knocked on the head from behind before she was strangled by hand. Whoever did it was wearing gloves. The killer didn't leave behind any physical evidence."

"So it was planned ahead of time," I said.

Murder in the first degree.

"No question."

"I'm surprised she was using hard drugs. She was a health food and fitness lover on the show." Proving once again that you can create a TV character for anybody and people will believe it's the real person. I asked, "What have you got on Nick Roma?"

Shaw and Jimmy exchanged looks. Shaw said, "He was the last one she texted that night. She was supposed to meet him at the restaurant at Dow's Lake."

"Nick said that he was there but she never showed." I made my voice sound bored—as if they had no proof of anything. "What else have you got?"

Jimmy couldn't hold back any longer. "Everyone says that Nick wanted to get back with her. Lena told the other models that she let him know they could only be friends. She also said that someone from her past was bothering her." He watched me as he spoke. "Jealous anger is a motive in my book."

"So again, no real evidence," I said, staring back. I thought about yawning to show how unimpressed I was but held back. Jimmy already had that stubborn look on his face that he got when he was sure he was right.

Shaw drew our attention back to him. "With luck, it's just a matter of time. I'm hoping you'll share whatever you find out, Sweet. Because I know you're digging, and Roma works for you. It won't go well if you try to protect him."

"I'll tell you when I have evidence of the real killer," I said, setting my coffee cup on the desk and standing up. "But you have to take off your blindfold and look at all the suspects, not just Nick Roma. Otherwise, your case against him will fold like a house of cards."

I left them without promising anything. I'd managed not to let on how worried I was that Nick really was guilty. I was going to keep searching until I had proof one way or the other. However, unlike Jimmy, I wanted Nick to be innocent. I needed to know that what I'd started to feel for him wasn't based on lies.

CHAPTER SEVEN

I parked in the oversized driveway of the model house and surveyed the yard through the steadily falling rain. The police cars were gone and the grey brick appeared gloomy under the low black clouds. The front yard looked naked with all the trees removed and interlocking stone instead of grass. The property was large but had no personality. Not a bit of homey warmth to be found.

As I watched, the front door opened. Director John Shore stepped outside and right behind him was the writer, Raymond Martel. I'd learned his full name from a list of crew I'd found on the internet. They stood talking on the front steps under the protection of the sloped roof. I got out of my car and hurried toward them. They stopped talking and watched me climb the steps to stand in front of them.

"Not filming today?" I asked.

Shore shook his head. "I decided to give the girls a day off. They're a little out of sorts with all that's been going on. We're bringing in a new model right after Thanksgiving weekend to liven the house up again."

"I'm sure that will help." *How shallow are you people?* "What country is she from?"

Shore squinted at me as if trying to remember where he'd seen me before. He paused before saying, "France. Raymond worked with her a few years ago."

"Did you know that Lena was using drugs?" I asked.

They exchanged looks before Shore said, "Nearly everyone in this industry uses something. Whatever she was into didn't affect her work."

I looked at Raymond. "Do you agree?"

"Yeah. Lena always delivered." I could have sworn he smiled before he turned away. He stepped around me to leave. Shore pushed himself past me and put himself squarely in my path, blocking my escape down the stairs.

"The girls are home but not taking company," Shore said. "And since you're not a cop, you're not welcome here today. In fact, you're not welcome here tomorrow either." His eyes had turned an icy shade of blue. He'd obviously just remembered who

I was, and someone must have let slip that I was a PI. "Bad things can happen to people who poke their noses in where they don't belong."

My heart started pounding harder in my chest and sweat beaded on my forehead. "That sounded like a threat."

"You can take it any way you want." He came closer, until my face was level with his chest. "Now get off this property." He reached out and shoved me backwards. I stumbled. It took a few seconds for me to regain my balance. Shore took another step toward me but I'd had enough. I scooted past him without saying anything and and ran down the steps. I walked quickly back to my car and he followed close on my heels. If he was trying to scare me, it was working. Shore watched while I got into my car. After I turned on my engine, he sauntered over to an idling BMW with Raymond behind the wheel.

I started driving slowly down the driveway. A moment later, the BMW zipped past me, both men laughing with their mouths wide open. I pulled out and turned in the opposite direction, driving slowly up the street. I checked my rear view mirror several times until I saw that they'd turned the corner. I made a U-turn and parked a few houses down from the model house. A full ten minutes passed while I waited to make sure they didn't come back. The time out gave me a chance to push back my fear and to stop my hands from shaking. Then I got out of my car and ran through the pouring rain to the front door.

••••••••••

I rang the bell and after a few minutes of no response, I tried the handle. The door opened and I stepped inside. I retraced my path to the back room where I'd found Sang Hee and Ella sitting on the couch the day before. I heard voices as I got closer, a man and a woman in a loud discussion. I stopped walking and listened just outside the doorway.

"I'm sure my contract says I don't have to do some of the things they're asking. Especially not this."

I recognized Sang Hee Yum's Korean accent. She sounded upset.

"We'll do the grieving thing for a few shows while I get over Lena. Then I'll start comforting you. It'll seem natural when we get together."

The man's voice must belong to Lena's pretend boyfriend, Dan Meech. I took a peek around the corner. They were sitting on the couch next to each other with their backs to me. They appeared to be holding scripts, likely for the next episode of the show.

"I don't know," Sang Hee said. "It seems too soon to me. My fans might not buy it."

"No need to worry. We can pull it off. How's Ella doing with . . . everything?"

"She went to the spa for the day to take her mind off Lena. She's flying to Mexico on Saturday for a shoot."

"We all need to take our minds off Lena. I think a new relationship between you and me will help viewers get over her death."

A door opened behind me and I turned to see a man in work clothes mopping the hallway. He spotted me and stopped what he was doing to stare. I took a step forward as if I was on my way into the living room. The man kept watching me so I continued walking into the room until I reached the couch. Two startled sets of eyes looked up at me. Sang Hee recognized me and her face relaxed.

"Hi," I said. I smiled at Sang Hee before saying to Dan, "You must have been Lena's boyfriend on the show. So sorry for your loss."

"Yeah. I'm Dan Meech. I got written into the script a month ago. They were trying to boost ratings." He had broad shoulders and blond good looks. The perfect hunky leading man if I'd ever seen one. "Such a tragedy."

"I'm sure you're going to miss her."

"Yeah. We had something special going on."

"Did you ever think about becoming her boyfriend for real?"

Dan gave me a curious look. "Not on your life. She wasn't my type." He paused and his eyes narrowed. "Who are you again?"

"Just one of the people helping out with the investigation."

He frowned. "I thought the killer was already under arrest."

"Not yet, but we're working on it." By the suspicious look in Dan's eyes, it seemed like a good time to make my exit. "Well, been nice meeting you," I said as I turned to leave.

Sang Hee stood up in one swift movement. "If you'll excuse me, I'm going to lie down. We can practise our lines later." She glanced at Dan and hurried ahead of me out of the room.

"Everything okay?" I asked when we reached the hall.

Sang Hee turned. Her beautiful black eyes were troubled. "Of course. Does John Shore know you've come back here?"

"Probably not."

She studied me for a moment before turning and walking in front of me to the bottom of the stairs. Then she turned, one hand on the banister. "You should be careful," she said softly. "Lena was scared for a reason." Then she ran up the stairs and out of sight.

I left the house and pulled out my cellphone as I reached my car. The conversations this morning had given me lots to think about and more digging to do. I would begin with a second visit to Nick Roma. I knew he had more information about Lena Caruso and it was time he shared it. That is, if he wanted me to help him stay out of prison.

CHAPTER EIGHT

Nick didn't answer his phone. Jada answered hers, but she had no idea where to find him. I hung up and thought for a minute. Then I phoned Roma's pizzeria. Gino picked up.

"Gino, it's Anna Sweet. I'm trying to find Nick."

"Anna. Thank goodness you're working on my boy's case. Nicky would never harm a hair on that girl's head. He's a good boy, my Nicky."

"Do you know where he is?"

"He's staying at my house in Little Italy. Twenty-two Oak Street. You go there now and I'll send over a pizza. A large with the works. Extra cheese. You want anchovies?"

"Sure, why not. I should be at your house in twenty minutes."

"Tell Nick he has to eat something. You'll find some red wine on the counter next to the fridge. Help yourself."

"Thanks Gino."

"Take care of him, Anna. He's not in a good way. I'm worried for him."

Nick has given us all reason to be worried for him.

The rain had stopped and the sun was peeking out when I drove east into Little Italy. Gino lived in a three-storey red brick house that faced a school and a soccer field. The homes on the street were close together, with front porches and tiny backyards. This was a neighbourhood where people knew each other and shared long summer evenings outside.

It took Nick a full five minutes to answer the door. By then, I was leaning on the doorbell.

He held onto the door with one hand and filled the opening. He was wearing a white undershirt and jeans, his feet bare. His hair was uncombed and dark circles were under his sad black eyes. "What do you want, Anna?" he asked.

"I have more questions."

"I'm not really up for company."

"I know. But this is important."

Nick looked at me for a long time. Long enough for my heart to start beating faster and my face to flush. He had a way of looking at me that made me feel as if he could see what I was thinking. At last, he opened the door wider and stepped aside to let me by.

We walked into the kitchen at the back of the house. It was a surprisingly sunny room for an old building. The walls were lined with tall oak cupboards and the latest cooking appliances sat on the granite counter top. A pine table stood under a hanging stained glass lamp. I found the wine and a couple of glasses and sat down across from Nick. He'd already taken a seat at the table and started working on a half-finished crossword puzzle. It looked like I'd interrupted him. I poured two glasses of wine and pushed one in front of him.

"Why did you really break up with Lena?" I asked.

"We'd grown apart." He said the words without energy, not looking up from the crossword puzzle.

"So you already said." I paused. "Now tell me the real reason."

He took his time filling in a word on the puzzle before he set his pen down. Then he took a deep breath and slowly let it out before staring across the table at me. "We were young. Moved in together when we were just eighteen years old and broke up less than two years later. We *had* grown apart. Lena wanted a jet set life with constant parties, shopping, and excitement. I liked reading, biking, and camping when I wasn't making a movie. I could have changed for her, I suppose. But I didn't like the person she was becoming, or the new friends she brought home. I moved to Venice for a summer to film a movie and didn't go back."

"How did she take it?"

"Lena was angry at first, and worried about her career. She felt that her image would be damaged if word got out that I dumped her. That never mattered to me so I told her to say she split up with me. After a year, Lena tried to start back up with me, but I wasn't interested. She moved to Ottawa several months back and tried again. She said that she wanted to get out of the life she'd made for herself. She knew now what was important."

"She was very beautiful."

"I'd moved on."

"Was Lena taking drugs when you were together?"

He hesitated, then said, "At the end, yes."

"Would you recognize any of her friends from back in Italy?"

Nick shook his head. "I didn't have much to do with them."

The doorbell rang and I jumped up to get the pizza. The smell made me light-headed—I hadn't eaten all day. I served up cheesy slices and refilled our wine glasses. I was happy to see Nick take a few bites of the piece I'd set in front of him.

I started putting my ideas together out loud. "Something happened to make Lena want out of her lifestyle. She was talking about leaving the show. She wanted to get back with you."

Nick said, "She told me that she did. But I think she just wanted to go back in time and start over. I reminded her of a simpler time, when she was happy."

I finished my first piece of pizza and took another out of the box. "She told someone from the show that a person from her past life was bothering her. If it wasn't you, then we have to figure out who it was. Because that's likely the person who killed her."

The doorbell rang again, but Nick didn't make any move to stand up.

"I'll get it," I said. I walked to the front door and looked out the peephole. When I saw who was standing on the front porch, I wished that I'd stayed in my chair back in the kitchen.

Jimmy frowned at me when I pulled the door open. Another officer was a few feet behind him on the walkway.

"Fancy meeting you here," Jimmy said. "We've come to take your pal Nick in for more questioning."

"Why, have you found something new? Because you had nothing before."

Jimmy chewed on the inside of his cheek. Just when I thought he wasn't going to tell me anything, he said, "Nick deposited thirty thousand dollars into Lena Caruso's account two months ago. He gave her five thousand more the day before she was killed. The money came from an offshore account and it took some detective work to trace it to him. Looks like Lena was blackmailing him. Killing her might have seemed easier than paying the next demand."

I stepped aside and let Jimmy walk by me without putting up an argument. There was no point. Nick had held back on me and now he was going to have to explain himself to the police.

Not to mention, proving him innocent had just gotten thirty-five thousand times harder.

CHAPTER NINE

A strange car was in Dad's driveway when I made it home soon after eight o'clock that evening. Dad didn't like company as a rule. I sat in my car and tried to see if anything was out of order. My eyes landed on the darkened steps. The outside light above the front door wasn't turned on. Dad always turned it on. I got out of my car and walked up to the house, uneasy about what I might find.

The front door was unlocked and I quietly stepped into the front hall. Thumping noises were coming from the living room. It sounded like somebody was being thrown about. I could feel nervous energy building inside me. If somebody was hurting my dad, they'd soon regret it. I crept along the wall until I reached the doorway where I eased my body into position, keeping out of sight. I tensed my legs, and lunged forward into the room.

Dad had his back to me, his arms wrapped around a woman in a blue silk dress. A second woman was turning up the music on Dad's ancient stereo. "I'm not sure I can lift you again," Dad said as he spun his partner around. He spotted me in mid-stride, my mouth hanging open. The woman looking after the stereo saw me and turned the music back down. She had snow white hair and was wearing a sparkly black dress.

"There you are," Dad said. "Norma, Betty, and I were just practising for the dance contest at the end of the month. Ladies, meet my eldest daughter, Anna. She's the PI that I told you about, working a case."

"How do you do?" I said.

"Your dad has said so many nice things about you, dear," Betty said, stepping back from Dad's side. She had permed white hair with a blue tint and a pleasant face. "He's very proud of you."

"He is?" The words were out of my mouth before I could stop myself. Dad never complimented me if he could help it. I added, "Well, isn't he turning into a big softie."

I glanced at my dad. A reddish flush had crept up his neck. He was looking at the floor.

I thought about high-fiving him but didn't want to add to his agony. "Well, please carry on," I said. "I have some work to do before bed."

"Some apple pie in the fridge," Dad said grudgingly, "in case you're hungry."

"Thanks, Pop."

Laughter and loud music followed me down the hall to the kitchen. I had mixed feelings about Dad's new lady friends. I was happy that he was having a good time. But I wasn't used to seeing him with a woman in his arms. His new social life added to my fear that the entire world as I knew it was hanging by a thread.

I ate a piece of pie standing in front of the kitchen sink, looking out the window while I thought over the day. Why had Nick paid so much money to a woman he was not dating? Why hadn't he told me about it? He must have known that the money would be traced back to him. I had to be missing something important. I returned to the fridge and cut another piece of pie to take upstairs to bed. A second helping of Dad's baking was turning into the high point of my day.

··········

Nick spotted me as soon as he walked out of the Ottawa Police station the next morning. I was leaning against the side of the building, waiting for him.

"Another long night?" I asked when I reached him on the sidewalk.

"You could say." He rewarded me with a tired smile.

"I've come to drive you home. But first, we need to talk."

He started walking and I fell into step beside him. "Maybe it's time."

We headed up Elgin Street on foot until we reached a restaurant that served a cheap breakfast. A table in front of the window was free so we sat and ordered bacon and eggs. I didn't ask Nick any questions until we'd each drunk a cup of coffee. To do otherwise would have been cruel after the sleepless night he'd put in.

"So, why did you deposit money in Lena's account?" I sat back and waited for Nick to explain. He set down his coffee mug and leaned his elbows on the table.

"I'm counting on you to keep what I am about to tell you out of the press."

I nodded. "This is between you and me. We're like a lawyer and a client, so I don't have to tell anybody anything."

Nick studied me for a minute. Then he said, "Lena got herself into trouble after we broke up.

She was travelling a lot for modelling shoots and started carrying drugs and money in her luggage. She stole thirty thousand dollars, thinking the drug dealer wouldn't notice. About a month ago, this person turned up asking for the money back."

"So you helped out."

"She was desperate and sorry for what she'd done. She wanted to start over. I had the money and could afford to give it to her."

"Do you know the name of the dealer?"

"No, but they had no reason to kill her. She'd paid up. Lena had as much to lose as they did if the truth came out."

"Why didn't you tell me this before?"

"I didn't want Lena's reputation destroyed. She made mistakes, but she wasn't a terrible person." Nick looked me directly in the eyes as he spoke. "I guess that I got used to protecting her."

"Sounds like you still cared for her."

"Not like you think. Lena had a rough childhood and missed out on normal family life. She spent her life trying to get over the emotional abuse." He paused. "And there's one more thing."

"What?"

"She made a movie, I think in France. She was taking drugs at the time and barely remembered doing it. She was terrified that the movie would be posted somewhere."

"We're talking porno movie?"

"Yeah. That's why she agreed to move the drugs and money when she was modelling. The dealer held the movie over her head. Said it would be posted everywhere if she didn't do what he asked. She believed her career would be ruined. She was only nineteen and wasn't able to handle the nastiness of the movie critics . . . or blackmail. When we were together, my success was like salt in her wounds."

I thought for a bit. "What about the five thousand you gave Lena a few days ago?"

"She was going to buy a ticket back to Italy. She promised me that she was giving up the high life and settling down. She had a job lined up in Milan in the fashion industry. She hated the reality TV show and wanted to go home."

"Did you share this information with the police just now?"

"I didn't tell them about the porno movie or her illegal activities. I told them I paid her the money as a favour."

"You know they're building a case against you."

"I know. I'm not willing to throw Lena to the wolves unless I really have to. Even though she's dead, I can't destroy her reputation. It was all she had left. Hopefully, you'll sort this out before that has to happen."

I looked at him and blinked a few times. Maybe it was the beginning of a nervous tick. Did he have any idea how much trouble he was in? I had to respect his strong sense of loyalty. But it was leading him to ruin as sure as we were heading for a winter deep freeze in a few short months.

• • • • • • • • • •

I called Jada as soon as I dropped Nick off at his father's house. I filled her in on the latest developments and asked her to do some research for me. I had an idea that might crack the case open. Call it a French connection. Jada agreed to get right on it. After hanging up, I got back on the highway and returned to the model house. A parking spot was free across the street behind a van. I slid my car into the spot and turned off the engine.

I stayed in my car for a while, watching members of the film crew go in and out the front door. I recognized a cameraman standing with another guy on the lawn. They were taking a smoke break. The director, John Shore, came out at one point, talking on his cellphone. I slumped in my seat and he didn't appear to see me.

An hour later, Jada called me back. I answered and held my breath.

"You were right," she said, "But how could you possibly have known? Are you a mind reader or what?"

I pumped my fist. *Yes!* "Things people said—I put them together."

"You have a knack for this work, you do know that, Anna Sweet? How are you going to get him to talk?"

"I'll present him with my evidence and see where it leads. Can you call Jimmy and fill him in? I'll set up a meeting and you both can come listen. I have my recording device, too."

"Will do, girl. You just make sure you keep yourself safe."

"Don't worry about me, partner. My going-it-alone hero days are long over."

CHAPTER TEN

I made it to the coffee shop early and was glad to see it was nearly empty. I set up my microphone on the table next to mine, which was littered in wrappers and coffee cups. The staff had agreed not to clean up the table to keep people from sitting there. Jada and Jimmy had a spot by the windows— Jada facing the door and Jimmy with his back to me because he could be recognized. Jada hadn't met anyone involved in the case, so she wasn't going to make our suspect suspicious.

At exactly five after five, my man walked through the door. He took a slow look around and then got in line for a coffee. After adding cream to his cup, he sauntered over to my table as if he hadn't a care in the world. He slid into the seat across from me.

"Fancy meeting you here."

"Glad you could make it, Raymond Martel," I said. "Or should I call you by your real name, Marcel Renaud? I imagine changing it was a good idea when you got out of prison. Clever to use the same first initials but in reverse."

He looked across at me and smiled. "Let's go to another table. Leave your bag and coat on the chair."

"Why?"

"Just being careful. I have a thing about being recorded."

"Sure, why not?"

I stood and he moved right behind me. His hands patted me down. In case anyone was watching, he said, "I'll find the keys. You have your hands full."

He was searching for an electronic device and I was glad I hadn't agreed to wear one when Jimmy asked. "Satisfied?" I asked when his hands slid away.

Then I walked over to another table. "Will this do?" I'd picked one on the other side of the dirty table with the microphone. It would still be able to pick up our conversation.

"Yeah, good enough."

We took seats across from each other. The table was small and our knees touched. I pulled mine back as if I'd rubbed against something gross.

"I haven't done anything illegal," he said. "I paid my debt to society for dealing drugs. I haven't returned to the business since I got out of prison. You've got nothing on me."

"You can't tell me that you started working on *A Model Life* by chance. You got a new identity so you could get into Canada because Lena was on the show. You tracked her down."

"I got offered the writing job to spice up the show. I've been doing exactly what the director wanted."

"Shower scenes? Make-out sessions? Women prancing around in their underwear?"

"That stuff boosts the ratings. Nobody else complained. I think Lena even liked it." Raymond's mouth twisted into a nasty grin.

"Why follow Lena to Canada after all this time?"

"She owed me some money."

"From your illegal drug business. You also were blackmailing her with a video you made back in France. Where's the video now?"

"I've got it. I'm talking to people about releasing it later this year. Before people forget Lena Caruso's name."

"You're disgusting."

"A guy has to make a living." He cracked the knuckles on his left hand one by one, watching me squirm the entire time. I swallowed my disgust.

"Is that why you killed her? Was she standing in the way of the film's release?"

Raymond held up a swollen finger. "Whoa there, madam. I never said I killed her. Why would I do that? She paid me what she owed me. She promised more if I destroyed the film. I told her that I was thinking about it, and I was. Now that she's dead . . . what's the harm in putting it out there for the world to see?"

"She had a lot on you, too. Illegal entry into Canada. Drug dealer, excuse me, ex–drug dealer, blackmailer . . ."

Raymond's eyes went dead cold. He spoke as if he could barely control the anger pulsing through him. "But not killer. And I'll deny everything we talked about today. In fact, I never heard of this Marcel Renaud person you've dreamed up. You'll not be able to prove anything."

Our eyes locked for a split second and fear filled me. The hatred on his face shook me worse than any ugly thing he could have said.

I started to get up, but Raymond shoved the table hard into my stomach and I buckled over. At the same time, he jumped to his feet and began running. I heard Jimmy scream "Stop!" as Raymond lurched past me. He made it to the entrance before Jimmy grabbed him. I held onto my aching stomach, picked up my recording device, and stumbled after

Jada to the door. We were in time to hear Jimmy say, "Get against the wall and hands behind your back. Now, you piece of scum!"

I felt Jada's arm go around me and I leaned into her. Jimmy looked back at us after he clicked handcuffs onto Raymond's wrists.

"You okay, Sweet?" he asked.

"I'll live." I tried taking a deep breath and felt a stab of pain in my belly. "Just get him out of here."

"My pleasure." Jimmy yanked on Raymond Martel's arm and shoved him toward the parking lot. "Congratulations, Mr. Martel or should I say Mr. Renaud? You've just made yourself the number one suspect in Lena Caruso's murder."

CHAPTER ELEVEN

It was another long night. Jada and I hung around the police station until midnight and then decided to go home. By then, Raymond had admitted to everything except killing Lena. Shaw and Jimmy put him in a cell and waited for a judge to sign a search warrant. They were hoping to find evidence at Raymond's apartment that would link him to the murder.

I met Jimmy in the hall on my way out of the station. He said, "Looks like you were right about Nick Roma. Much as I hate to be proven wrong." The regret in Jimmy's face was probably because Nick was no longer a suspect. Not because he'd misjudged him.

"Good thing you kept an open mind," I said, deadpan. "Well, see you at Dad's for supper on Sunday. Turkey with all the fixings. I'm taking my aching stomach home to bed."

• • • • • • • • • •

I took the next day off. Lay in bed until noon reading a detective novel. Uploaded and watched three movies on my computer. Then met Jada for a late supper at the Flying Banzini, a local sandwich and pizza restaurant.

"Raymond Martel, otherwise known as Marcel Renaud, still hasn't confessed to the murder." Jada took a bite of her roast chicken and bacon panini and moaned with pleasure. "The lemon-chive mayo really brings out the flavour. Heaven." She licked her fingers. "Any word from Nick?"

"No."

"Probably taking a day to recover from the stress. He said he'd be back at work after Thanksgiving weekend."

"Great." I took a bite of my roast beef pizza. The horse radish gave it just the right zing. I put my fork on the table. "Do you think . . . do you think Nick really is innocent?"

"Of course!" Jada frowned at me. "How can you doubt him?"

"I doubt everyone." I met her eyes. "It's just that I got the feeling Raymond was telling the truth when he said he wasn't the killer. And Jimmy said they came up empty in their search of his house."

"A feeling isn't proof. And Raymond had lots of time to get rid of any evidence."

"I guess." I picked up my fork. Usually when a case finished up, the worry bees in my stomach settled down. They hadn't yet. Maybe I'd been working too hard and didn't know how to relax. I said, "I think I'll take tomorrow off, too. That'll give me a five-day break, including Thanksgiving Monday. I need some time to recharge."

"No problem. I'm going to drop by the office tomorrow to do some paper work. I might take Friday afternoon off too. We've both earned a holiday."

· · · · · · · · · ·

I really had intended to take Friday off. But at ten o'clock the next morning, I was sitting in my car across the road from the model house, drumming my fingers on the steering wheel. Why couldn't I let this case go? Nick was in the clear and Raymond Martel was the logical killer. Every clear-thinking person would agree . . . But having another poke around couldn't hurt, could it? Unless I found new evidence that pointed back to Nick.

That would be bad. Very bad.

I saw some of the film crew go in the front door. I walked up the driveway and slipped inside the house after them. My blue nylon windbreaker and jeans helped me to fit in, as did a Blue Jays ball cap with my hair tucked inside. I found an out-of-the-way spot to watch the models in action. I made sure to stay out of John Shore's line of sight. Luckily, he was busy directing and had his back to me. Someone called out for Martel to rewrite a sentence.

Shore said, "Raymond called a few hours ago. He's not well and needed the day off. We'll have to make do without him today."

So Raymond Martel hadn't admitted to being arrested. Or Shore was covering for him. *Interesting.*

The first action scene had Ella and Sang Hee pretending to tidy up the living room. They were chatting about the new model who was set to arrive next episode. Then came a discussion about nail polish colours. After a couple of hours of reshooting the same conversation, the crew shifted outside to the back deck. By then, I felt just this side of brain dead.

The models disappeared upstairs. Ten minutes later, Sang Hee came back wearing a bright blue bikini that showed off her perfect body.

"Ella asked if she can leave for the airport," she said to Shore.

"I'm finished with her for today. Where's Meech?" He looked around and I moved behind a tropical plant.

"Coming." Dan Meech stepped into the room along with a woman dabbing powder on his face. He was wearing tight black swim trunks, with his muscles flexing all over the place. "I hope that the hot tub is up to temperature."

"Hot enough to fry fish." Shore followed Sang Hee, Dan, and the film crew outside onto the deck.

I scooted into the hallway and up the stairs. I slipped through an open bedroom door, barely missing Ella pulling her suitcase down the hall. She stopped on the landing at the head of the stairs to answer her cellphone.

Her voice travelled to my hiding spot. "I can't wait to get out of here for a few days. It was hard enough having Lena die. Now, I spend half my time trying not to punch you-know-who in the face." She paused and said, "Yeah, creepy as ever. This set is toxic." She took a few steps down. "Okay, I'll call you tonight after I land. Sure. Love you too."

She started down the stairs. I looked around the room I'd stepped into. It was a large bedroom with a king-size bed and mirrors lining one wall. The closet was empty, as was the attached bathroom. This must have been Lena's room. I did a quick search in case anything had been missed, but found nothing.

I checked out the other two identical bedrooms at the end of the hall. Clothes, shoes, makeup, and jewellery confirmed that the rooms belonged to Ella and Sang Hee. I searched both, not sure what I was looking for and not finding it. I checked my phone. I'd been upstairs over an hour.

I made it to the head of the stairs and peeked over the railing. Sang Hee was at the bottom and she was screaming mad. "I'm not doing another take! You can all go to hell." She raised her right middle finger to somebody before stomping up the stairs. She was clutching onto a beach towel and her hair was dripping wet.

I ducked back inside the empty bedroom just in the nick of time.

CHAPTER TWELVE

I wanted to leave but the crowd of people at the bottom of the stairs kept me in place. It sounded like the crew was packing up and the front door opened and shut several times. Sang Hee didn't leave her bedroom the entire time.

At last, the noise downstairs stopped. I waited a few more minutes before leaving the bedroom and walking on tiptoe to the head of the stairs. The sound of car engines got fainter as the crew drove away. I listened for anyone downstairs. I almost jumped into the wall when I saw Dan Meech step out from behind the French doors. He was dressed in jeans, a black T-shirt, and running shoes, but his hair was still wet from the hot tub. He didn't see me and I raced back to the bedroom. I could hear his footsteps on the stairs, but only because I was listening for them. My door was slightly open and I chanced a look into the hall.

Dan was outside Sang Hee's bedroom door. He tried the handle slowly, and found it locked. He took a look around the hall and I pulled back into the shadows. A moment later I peeked again, and he was quietly dragging a chair from the sitting area at the end of the hall closer to Sang Hee's door. She wouldn't see him if she looked outside her room.

I was starting to get a really bad feeling.

I couldn't leave now even if I wanted to. Meech sat himself down and waited for Sang Hee to come out of her room. She was in no hurry and an hour crept by.

Something moved in my pocket. My phone! Thank goodness I'd put it on vibrate. I pulled it out and looked at the number. *Jimmy*. I didn't dare answer. Besides, he was the last one I wanted to tell that I'd snuck into the model house. But his call gave me an idea.

I scrolled to Jada's number and typed a text message, giving her my current situation. I suggested I might need help. A few seconds later, my phone vibrated again. She was on her way. Twenty minutes, tops.

It was less than ten minutes later when Sang Hee opened her bedroom door. I scooted back to my post in time to see her step into the hall. She was almost at the head of the stairs when Meech grabbed her from behind and pulled her neck back against his chest. She let out a shriek.

"My love," Dan said, and kissed her cheek before letting her go.

Sang Hee turned to face him, rage filling her face. "What . . . are . . . you . . . doing . . . here?" Each word a bullet of anger.

Dan didn't appear to notice that she wasn't happy to see him. "I thought we could spend the evening together. We can share a bottle of wine . . ."

"Are you out of your mind? I'm not sharing anything with you. In fact, I've told Shore that either you're off the show, or I am."

His forehead crinkled up and his eyes showed he was puzzled. "I don't understand. You kissed me in the hot tub. I could tell it was real."

Sang Hee was losing control. "You're a creep. How much clearer do I have to be? Stop following me around. Stop acting like we're a couple in real life. No wonder Lena wanted you gone. She was just too nice to make you lose your job, but not because she didn't want to." Sang Hee shoved the palm of her hand against Dan's chest.

The confusion in his eyes turned to anger. "Lena was a liar and a cheat. She told me that she loved me but she was meeting that Nick Roma behind my back."

"She told you because she had to for the show. Are you insane?" Then Sang Hee's eyes went wide. For the first time, I heard a hint of fear in her voice. She whispered, "What did you do?"

"Women who cheat deserve what they get."

Sang Hee didn't respond. I could imagine the wheels were turning inside her head at a frantic pace. She must have realized that she was alone in the house with a killer. I could sense her terror because I was feeling some of it myself.

It seemed like a good time to make myself known. Before Dan had a chance to get nasty.

I pushed the door open and pretended to be talking loudly on my phone. "Sure. I'll have her there in half an hour. I think she wants the full waxing." I acted surprised to see the two of them in front of me. "Hey, Sang Hee. The spa is waiting for you. Dan, how are you, man?"

I marched over and grabbed Sang Hee by the arm. "Let's get moving. You're already late and you know they charge extra if you waste their time."

"Of course." Her eyes thanked me, but the look of terror was still on her face. We started at a half-jog down the stairs.

"I've called 9-1-1," I whispered. "The police will be here any minute."

Dan Meech hurtled down the stairs as if he'd been shot from a cannon. He shoved me in the back before we reached the bottom step. I staggered and let go of Sang Hee as I hit the wall. Sang Hee tumbled ahead of me down the last step, banging her head against the banister before sprawling flat out on the floor. Pain shot through my shoulder but I could still move my arm. Meech pushed me again and I flew over the last step, landing next to Sang Hee. Her eyes were closed and she wasn't moving.

Before I could help her, Meech grabbed me— luckily by my good arm—and pulled me to my feet. "You couldn't leave us alone. You're the reason everything has gone wrong." He pulled back his hand and made a fist that was lined up with my face.

Before he could unload, I jabbed my knee upward as hard as I could between his legs. I felt something crunch and it was Meech's turn to stagger back. He let go of me and dropped onto the floor, holding onto himself and rolling about in pain. He was blocking my exit so I tried to jump over him. But his hand grabbed onto my ankle and held on like a vice grip.

"Let go of me." I tried to shake him off and lost my balance. My chin hit the floor and for a moment, I saw stars. I felt Meech crawl on top of me and then his hands were around my neck.

"You're going to pay for what you've done," he said, lifting my head and banging it on the floor. Not once but twice. Then he squeezed my throat, cutting off my air. I clawed at his arms with my hands.

Meech was so busy choking me that he didn't hear the front door open. He realized too late that Jada was running full tilt toward us. She had the look of a woman about to do battle to the death. Meech let go of my neck but Jada's fist landed a knockout punch to his face before he could get his hands up to defend himself. His eyes rolled back and he dropped on top of me.

Jada shoved him sideways onto the floor and helped me into a sitting position. I sputtered and coughed until I felt air enter my lungs. After I took a few deep breaths, I pointed toward the stairs and croaked, "Sang Hee?"

We both looked over. Sang Hee was sitting up, holding her head.

Jada said, "You're both going to be okay. Medical help is right behind me."

The police picked that moment to rush in. They took over the downstairs and had Meech in handcuffs before he was fully awake. Sang Hee was hustled away in an ambulance but I refused to go. I finally let a paramedic look over my injuries in the living room after Jada and a police officer insisted.

"Thanks for getting here so quickly," I said to Jada after finding out nothing was broken. I'd have a swollen neck for a few days and my chin was going to be sore and purple. But not bad, considering. "You have quite the right hook, by the way."

"I've been known to punch above my weight class." Jada grinned. "Looks like making my mom put me in boxing class instead of ballet was a good call."

"I'll say. Remind me to send her a thank-you card."

CHAPTER THIRTEEN

"Couldn't you find a smaller turkey, Dad?" I leaned into the oven to baste the bird, which had to run twenty-five pounds. It was almost too big for the roasting pan.

"Thought I might invite a few more people." Dad was cutting green beans at the counter.

The front door opened. A few seconds later, Evan ran into the kitchen. "Aunt Anna, look what I got."

Dad and I hugged him before admiring his new remote-controlled airplane. "Do you want to fly it with me, Grandpa?"

"Sure do, kiddo. But not until after supper."

Jimmy and Cheri walked into the kitchen and more hugs followed. I hadn't seen Cheri since she got back from China. She looked good, with a short new haircut and stylish clothes. She smelled of spice and jasmine.

"I brought you a gift," she said, handing me a package. "I'm sorry I took so long to come see you."

I ripped open the paper and found a red silk dressing gown and matching slippers from China. "They're beautiful," I said and gave her another hug. "It's good to have you home."

Cheri glanced over at Jimmy. By the look on his face, I could tell they'd been fighting. Jimmy turned toward Dad and held up a bottle of wine that they'd brought. "Pour anyone a glass?"

"I think we could all use a drink," Dad said.

The doorbell rang and Dad sent me to let more people in. Jada and her younger brother Henry were at the door. We had just made it to the kitchen when the doorbell rang again. I returned to find Gino and Nick Roma on the steps. "Your dad kindly invited us to share your meal," Gino said. "How could we say no on such a happy day?"

I hugged Gino and looked over his shoulder at Nick. He looked tired but smiled at me. I smiled back but my stomach felt slightly sick. I wondered how to get past the guilt I felt for having believed he could be the killer.

The last guest to arrive was Dad's new dance partner, Betty, making us an even ten for Thanksgiving dinner. Betty took my place in the kitchen, helping

Dad finish up the last of the cooking. Somehow, it felt right.

The next few hours flew by as we dug into turkey and stuffing, mashed potatoes, and pumpkin pie. There was much laughter and chatter, but we steered away from talk about Lena's murder after Jimmy said Dan Meech had confessed. Nick was quieter than the rest of us, but he joined in now and then. Jimmy kept looking over at him but didn't go out of his way to be friendly.

After pie and coffee, and time in the backyard with Evan's plane, our guests started to say their goodbyes. Nick was the only one to remain behind. Dad came into the kitchen where we were sitting at the table. He looked at Nick and said, "I'm heading to bed now with a nightcap. Either of you want a splash of whiskey?"

"We're good, Dad."

"Well, good night, kids. Don't forget to lock up, Anna."

"I will."

After the door to Dad's room shut, Nick and I put on our jackets and went outside to watch the stars. We dragged two lawn chairs to the centre of the backyard and sat with our elbows touching.

"I'd like to take you to dinner, Anna," Nick said after a while. "If you'd still like to go."

I didn't feel right accepting. Guilt was holding me back. If he knew how long I'd suspected him of being the killer . . . "Nick, you need to know that I thought you might have killed Lena, right up to the end. I didn't want it to be you, but I didn't trust you. I'm sorry."

"And now?"

"Now? Now, I realize how loyal and good you are. I feel bad for having doubted you."

Nick was quiet for a moment. I felt my hope disappearing with every passing second. I was surprised and relieved when he reached over and held onto my hand.

"I would have been surprised if you had trusted me with so little to go on. I'm not an up-front kind of person, and neither are you. But now, I think we can start fresh and get to know each other."

My heart leapt up a bit, but not all the way. "There's one more thing you should know." I paused. The next part was probably the deal breaker. No matter how I framed my relationship with Jimmy in my head, it was going to come out wrong. I took a deep breath and turned to look at him. "My brother-in-law, Jimmy, and I were once engaged."

The patient look was back in Nick's eyes. "Jada told me all about it. Another reason for you not to trust me too quickly. But I'm not Jimmy. I won't make the mistake of giving you up."

And with that said, Nick leaned over and kissed me.

When he pulled away, I asked, "Is tomorrow night too soon for that dinner date? The turkey and pie should be worn off by then, I imagine."

Nick smiled and gently brushed the hair away from my forehead. "Tomorrow night can't come soon enough," he said.

And then, he leaned in and kissed me again.

ABOUT THE AUTHOR

 Brenda Chapman is a well-known mystery author. The Anna Sweet Mysteries are a popular series in adult literacy and English as a Second Language programs. *My Sister's Keeper*, the first title in the series, was a finalist for the Arthur Ellis Award in 2014. *The Hard Fall* was nominated for the Golden Oak Award in 2014. A former teacher, Brenda now works as a senior communications advisor in Ottawa.

ALSO BY BRENDA CHAPMAN

In Winter's Grip
The Second Wife
Second Chances
Cold Mourning
Butterfly Kills

Anna Sweet Mysteries
My Sister's Keeper
The Hard Fall
To Keep a Secret

Jennifer Bannon Mystery Series
Running Scared
Hiding in Hawk's Creek
Where Trouble Leads
Trail of Secrets

You can visit Brenda's website at
www.brendachapman.ca